The Seekers

The Way to Freedom

Book 6

H.M. Clarke

Sentinel Publishing

Copyright © H. M. Clarke 2017

All rights reserved; no part of this publication may be
reproduced or transmitted by any means, electronic, mechanical,
photocopying or otherwise, without the prior permission of the
copyright owner

First published in The United States of America in 2018

Sentinel Publishing LLC, Dayton, Ohio

Cover design by Deranged Doctor Design

The moral right of the author has been asserted

Also by H.M.Clarke

The Way to Freedom Series
1: The Kalarthri
1.1: The Cavern of Sethi
2: The Dream Thief
3. The Awakening
4. The Enemy Within
5. The Unknown Queen
6. The Searchers

The Complete Season One – Books 1-5

Coming soon
7. The Whisperer

John McCall Mysteries
1: Howling Vengeance

The Verge
1: The Enclave

Coming Soon
2: Citizen Erased

The Order/Ravensdale

1: Winter's Magic

Marion: An 'Order' Short Story

DEDICATION

As always, this book is dedicated to my two beautiful children, Keith and Ariadne.

CONTENTS

"Whoever destroys a soul, it is considered as if he destroyed an entire world. And whosoever that saves a life, it is considered as if he's saved an entire world."

-A Saying of the Pydarki

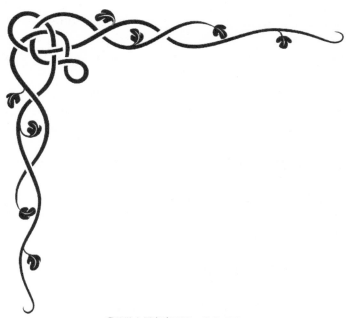

CHAPTER ONE

WAITING

Everything was still.

Everything was quiet.

Not even the air moved through the

branches of the close-packed conifers, firs and

larches.   The moon was full and glowed like pure

white porcelain and slowly climbed above the

horizon, gradually revealing the clear, midnight blue of the night sky above. The landscape was starkly silhouetted against the starlit night sky.

Through the trees could be heard the snoring of men, the occasional snort of a horse, the clink of metal as the dog watch sentry moved about their patrol of the camp.

Adhamhma'al'mearan moved his head carefully from under his black feathered wing and patiently surveyed the clearing around him. Both the Hatar'le'margarten slept a short way off from the main camp so that their presence would not frighten the Freemans horses.

Across the clearing from him, Trar slept with her head tucked loosely under her wing and her tail curled tightly around her front claws. She hated camping out of doors and missed the comforts of her soft fluffy leather bed in the Hatar Barracks at Darkon.

But at this moment Adhamh could sense that her consciousness was caught deep in sleep. He knew that she would not be waking in a hurry.

He and Trar were the only Hatar resting in this clearing tonight as the other two Hatar'le'margarten had been sent back to Fort Foxtern by Kral Tayme to report to Wing Commander Harada and Colonel Jan Oded about what was happening out here in the ranges.

Adhamh turned his gaze away from the sleeping Trar and focused his attention on the humans camped among the trees beyond them. After a few moments as the stillness reassured him that there would be no one coming to check on them, Adhamh slowly stood up and carefully folded his wings tightly to his body so that they would not catch on anything and make any undue noise.

He could not sleep, even though he was bone tired. His growing anxiety about Kalena was consuming his mind.

He hated this sitting and waiting.

He hated having to trail along after Freeman who did not care one twit about his missing Wingmate.

He hated that Kral Tayme keeping him here instead of letting him search the mountains for her.

Adhamh's Krytal Crystal felt like it was quickly vibrating behind his ear. It had started just before dusk and would not stop. That had Adhamh worried that Kalena was in danger; that her paired crystal was calling to him for help. He had to find her and staying with the humans was slowing his search for Kalena. It was time for Adhamh to leave and search for Kalena himself.

His gaze swept the clearing one, final time before he moved as quietly as his large frame would allow over to the cliff edge.

Taking a deep breath, Adhamh then spread his wings and walked off the precipice.

Adhamh then slipped upward into view as he started long, slow wing beats to steadily climb up into the midnight dark sky.

He was being called. And he could resist it no longer.

The thermal loosened its hold and Adhamh began to drop through the air. He pumped his wings in a large down sweep and felt himself quickly lift up to altitude. Until he can find the next thermal he will have to use his own power to stay where he needed to be.

Adhamh's eyes carefully roamed the landscape below him, constantly looking for any sign of what he was seeking. But something was drawing him towards the mountains. Something within him was leading him to Kalena.

Adhamh could feel the tickle of the Krytal crystal where it was embedded just behind his left ear. Maybe it was calling out to the matched crystal that was embedded behind Kalena's ear. Maybe the Krytal was what had been leading him into the Northern Mountains. Towards the stronghold of the Ice Tigers, and beyond the mountains lay Arran, a country that was not on a friendly footing with the Suene Empire.

Knowing my luck, Kalena is probably being

held by the Arranians. Their Spellcrafters might

have been able to knock me from the sky and take

her...if they had enough of them to combine their

power and focus it.

That was the only scenario that Adhamh

could come up with that logically explained how he

and Kalena could have been struck from the sky

that day. The Arranian Spellcrafters are one of the

only people with the Talent to do that, and even

though they are not as powerful as they once were,

a group of them working as one could theoretically

do this. Another Hatar'le'margarten could do this

as well, but Adhamh would have known the instant

he was hit if it was a fellow Hatar'le'margarten.

No. It had to be the Arranians. That is why

Adhamh was being lead north into the mountains.

Because beyond those mountains lie the kingdom of

Arran and hopefully Kalena.

These were the thoughts running constantly through Adhamh's mind since he awoke and found Kalena gone. Not just physically gone, but mentally as well. He had grown so used to their constant connection that when it was suddenly gone it felt as if he had been gutted. The ache of the emptiness throbbed deep down in Adhamh's head and chest. Because of this, he had resolved to do anything to get her back. Anything.

This is why he had crept away during the night and was now flying steadily north.

Adhamh was up high. High enough that his blue feathered underbelly would merge into the blue expanse of the sky and would be missed by any causal glance. The sky ran blue before him as far as the eye could see, only marred by the sloppy remains of the cloud bank that had passed through yesterday and was now clinging stubbornly in the north.

He took note of the Suenese troop movements, most of which were heading to Fort Foxtern, but there were two small groups that had broken away from the main force and were now moving north into the mountains. On the spur of the moment, Adhamh had decided to follow them as they were all going in the same direction. The Hatar was also curious about where they were heading. Maybe they were scouts or escorting one of the Emperor's spies to the edge of Arranian territory.

He drifted lazily, enjoying the feel of the warm sun against his back feathers. It was nice to be able to fly wherever you want without being under orders. It was also nice to be actually doing something constructive to find Kalena.

If anything had happened to her...

Adhamh turned his thoughts away from that direction. If he found Kalena with more than a scratch on her, he would not stop until he had hunted down and took his revenge on every last member of the party that captured her.

He corrected his course to head a little more north as his instinct guided him and then let the steady beat of his wings lull him into boredom.

It was early afternoon when he reached the foothills of the Bhaligier ranges. The thermals and air currents had begun to change as he approached the mountains and his wings began to have to work harder to get him where he needed to go.

Adhamh began to keep an eye out for a safe

and hidden place to spend the night. A hard thing to find when you are the size of a small house. The best he could hope for is a small clearing in the trees that covered the skirts of the mountains. Or if he was lucky, a cave.

A cave would be ideal. He could stay hidden and warm and have the secure feeling of having something 'heavy' around him. A cave would also be easier to defend....or get trapped in...Adhamh thought on that a few moments more before deciding. Does not matter, I still prefer a cave. He began to skirt around the mountains, looking for promising rock outcrops and plateaus.

The sun was low in the west when the glint of stone flashed pink in the late afternoon light. Adhamh focused his attention on it and saw that it was a large stone plateau that jutted out over a stand of conifers. A perfect place to spend the night. The only things that could reach him there were other flying creatures or the mountain goats or bighorn sheep – and even they aren't silly enough to get close to a Hatar'le'margarten that could swallow them in one bite.

The thought of sheep made Adhamh's stomach grumble. It was too late to hunt tonight, so he would have to keep his eye out tomorrow for game and maybe bag himself a couple of those sheep. That would keep him going for a couple more days.

Adhamh circled slowly down towards the grassy plateau, keeping a lazy eye on the scatter of birds that high tailed it away as fast as they could. He caught no sight of any large mammals hurrying away, which put paid to any thought of a quick and easy meal before bed.

He landed and made a quick inspection of the ground to make sure that all was safe and then went and curled up near the edge of the trees where they met the mountain face. Adhamh was utterly exhausted. Everything he had been though coupled with the days hard flying had drained him of what little energy reserves he had left in his body. He fell deeply asleep as the sky grew quickly into the midnight blue darkness of an early moonless night, knowing that his black, feathered form would just merge into the mountain in the darkness.

Adhamh abruptly awoke to complete silence.

He tried to get up but found himself held down somehow by his legs and tail. Then silently out of the darkness came ropes and hooks being thrown over his back, securing his wings tightly against his body. Adhamh made another effort to free himself but found that each time he struggled the bonds that held him just got tighter and tighter. He relaxed and slumped to the ground, best to keep what energy he had left for when he really needed it.

As soon as he relaxed, men started to appear out of the starlit darkness, holding the ends of the ropes and chains that now bound him. He curled his lip at them, baring his long teeth and had a smug feeling of satisfaction when a few of the men took an involuntary step backwards. Behind these men stood a small figure whose dark shape

24

stood out from the midnight blue of the night. He was quickly moving his arms and then suddenly noise rushed back into the void around Adhamh.

The man was a Spellcrafter. Adhamh had found the Arranians – or rather, the Arranians had found him.

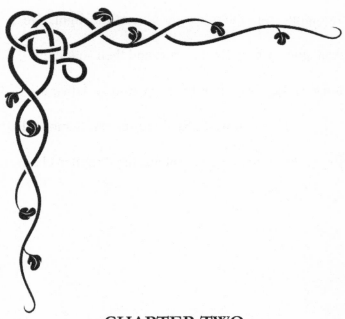

CHAPTER TWO

SURPRISE!

Dearen tugged her hat low over her face and crawled backwards from the edge of the cliff to join Hauga and the others hidden in the undergrowth.

'They are encamped just below us. Does everyone know what they have to do?'

Dearen looked at each furry face as the five

Dymarki with her gave their reply.

'Yes, Cearc.'

Dearen tried not to frown at the title. She had only been Cearc for a week and she was already getting too used to hearing Cearc attached to her name.

'Remember, surprise is the key to making this work.'

'We know Dearen. No need to tell us for the hundredth time. We are no longer cubs playing around our mother's feet.'

Dearen tired to hold back a smile.

'I don't know Hauga, sometimes you make me wonder if you are as old as you say you are.'

Suddenly Dearen's mind was filled with the mental sniggering of four of the Dymarki while Hauga gave a mental humph and turned his back to her.

'If you're finished trying to be funny, shall we begin?'

'Yes. Okay, everyone. Once we get into position, I'll give the signal and then we drop.'

'Yes, Cearc.'

'Very good,' Dearen thought as she looped her arms around Hauga's white furred neck and wrapped her legs around the Dymarki's waist as he stood.

Dearen looked at the scene below. It was evening twilight. The sun had just dipped behind the mountains, the people below had just finished making camp and were now busy preparing their evening meals with a single guard set at the mouth of the natural enclosure.

No one down below was looking for an

28

attack from above.

Targets had been picked by her and her Dymarki and Dearen sent a quick mental note to the five Dymarki to make sure they attack their marked target.

'Are we ready to go?' Hauga asked, impatience thick in his mental voice.

Dearen started to nod and then remembered that not everyone could see her.

'Yes. On the count of three we go.'

'Yes, Cearc.'

Dearen glanced once more along the line of the cliff face at the Dymarki concealed in the trees and undergrowth.

'One...two...' Dearen took one final breath and gripped tighter around Hauga's neck and shoulder. *'...three.'*

Dearen felt a lurch in her stomach as Hauga leaned forward and stepped off the edge of the cliff. Her stomach was then left behind as they both hurtled straight down to the clearing below.

Directly beneath them was a warrior standing by his bedroll, looking towards the campfire. He was not expecting to be attacked from above.

At the last instant, something must have warned him as the solider suddenly looked up in time to feel the weight of Hauga's body bound into him.

Dearen automatically released her hold and rolled away, letting Hauga dispatch the warrior with a mock slash of his claws.

She quickly looked around and saw that the other five had done their jobs and four more warriors were down. Dearen drew her wooden training blade and headed straight toward the command tent.

It was not really a tent, just a lean-to with a cloth thrown over it to protect its occupants from the wind and weather.

Dearen was coming up around the back of the tent when the head of one of its occupants poked itself around the corner. She immediately shoved the point of her wooden blade deep into the thick fur of the enemies neck. He let out a slow hiss and then turned ice blue eyes on Dearen.

Behind her, Dearen could hear excessive grunting and assumed that Hauga was dealing with the tent's other occupant.

Dearen kept the point of her wooden blade buried in the thick fur.

Flattened ears slowly twitched and the ice blue eyes began to twinkle.

'Good evening Cearc. I see that you got me again. Your timing is perfect as dinner is ready.'

Dearen could not help the grin that spread across her face as she pulled the practice sword away from the Dymarki's neck.

'How did you get us this time?' the patrol leader asked, rubbing a clawed hand on his neck.

"We got you from above." Dearen turned and pointed behind her. "We came down off of the cliff face."

'Do you really think the Arranians will fight the same way?'

"Do you want to take the chance?" Dearen countered. "We have not seen the Arranians in hundreds of years. Who can say how they will fight? You need to remember that they have Spellcrafters so we have to practice our guerilla tactics. A Spellcrafter taken by surprise has no chance to craft a spell against us have they?"

'No. I guess you're right.'

"We have to make sure that we are never caught by surprise ever again. We are not going to lose any more of our people without a fight, and we have to prepare ourselves if we want to fight well."

'Yes Cearc'

"Let's all go have dinner and we'll talk more about this afterwards. Tactics, strategy and repetition are what will help us win our mountains back."

'Enough with the grandstanding Dearen, and come and eat!'

Hauga's voice cut through into her

conversation and she turned to the campfire to see the Dymarki already seated on a tree stump with a trencher of meat already in his hands.

"It's only the quick and the dead around you isn't it Hauga."

'Only the quick get the best cuts of meat.'

"What is it with you and food?"

'I'm a growing cub and I need my sustenance, is what my mother always told me.'

"Mothers always indulge the ones they love – Maybe overindulge is more the word in your case," Dearen replied as she patted her hand on Hauga's belly.

Howls of Dymarki laughter, both mental and vocal, rose at her words.

Hauga curled his lips back in a smile of his own, letting the warm juices from the meat drip off of his sharp canines.

Dearen gave him a playful push and sat down on the stump beside him. Hauga handed her a plate of cut meats.

'Don't say that I never think of you.'

"I would never say that Hauga. You are the best brother a girl could ever ask for." Dearen saw Hauga's whiskers raise as he tried to fight back a smile. "Now. Don't get all mushy on me. Let's get eating before all this gets cold."

With grunts of agreement from the other Dymarki in camp, the group all sat down to eat.

Later that night, Dearen was laying in her tent with the furs of her sleeping roll pulled up to

under her chin. Night in the mountains was cold.
She could hear Hauga's gentle purring by the
entrance. Lately, he had taken to sleeping just
inside the tent entrance as an added line of defence
for the Cearc. The Dyamarki did not want to be
caught unawares again.

The rest of the camp had settled down for
the night apart from those that had guard duty. But
Dearen could not sleep. Her body felt bone tired
but her mind would not rest. She felt as if there was
something pulling at the back of her mind, calling to
her.

Calling to her for help.

The sensation felt familiar, comforting, a
part of her, though she could not remember feeling
it before.

Dearen shook her head and flipped over to

her side to see if lying in a different position would dispel the feeling. It did not.

As she lay, whatever the feeling was, grew more intense and she began to feel the urge to go North.

She had to head North.

The feeling was insistent. She had to head North without delay or bad things may happen.

Dearen pressed her eyes shut, trying to dispel the feeling and get some sleep. Maybe this was a part of her new powers? She made a mental note to talk about it to Hauga in the morning.

And with that thought, Dearen drifted into an uneasy sleep.

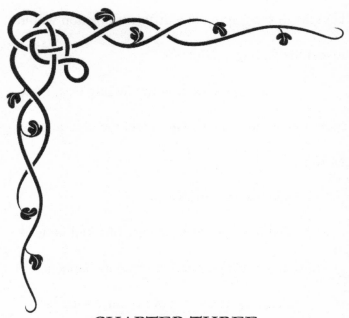

CHAPTER THREE

THE HUNT

'He was here'

Tayme immediately sat up in the saddle and began to scan the sky around him.

'He was? Can you tell if he is still close by?'

Trar let a whiff of exasperation come across

their link. *'I know I'm good, but I'm not that good.'*

'How can you tell he was here?'

Trar snorted. *'The clearing we just flew over has a flattened area where he had rested. He also relieved himself there. I can still smell it from way up here.'*

'Okay, Trar. I believe you. Do you have any idea which direction Adhamh headed in when he left?'

'I have no idea. But something does not seem right with that clearing.'

'We'd best meet up with those on the ground and check it out.'

'Do you think the Lieutenant still thinks that his missing Captain came this way as well?'

'With no trace of his Captain's tracks or scent heading out anywhere with no idea of

direction or motive, he doesn't have much choice,
now does he?'

Trar snorted and dipped her wing to turn
lazily around in the direction of the ground patrol.

'I still think you should have kept Jill or
Traer here with us.'

'Really? It's hard enough feeding and
hiding you with us much less have two more
Hater'le'margarten around to deal with.'

Trar snorted again but said nothing more.

She started gliding down the side of the
mountain towards the wooded valley below. Tayme
could see the small patrol lead by Lieutenant Dalon
Peana and his gangly tracker toiling through the
trees. The group was not making much effort to
remain hidden and Tayme assumed that it was
probably because of their close proximity to the

Pydarki stronghold of Daegourouf. But they were also close to the Northern border, the one shared with Arran. Not to mention the Ice Tigers that are supposed to be lurking in these mountains someplace. They could be hidden anywhere on these ranges and the Pydarki do not seem that concerned with keeping them out.

The Pydarki were not really a warlike people, but that does not explain their unconcern about letting the likes of the Ice Tigers and maybe the Arranians unfettered access to their ancestral lands.

'We are going to land ahead on the path Kral. Just watch that you don't get hit by a tree branch.'

'I'll be careful. Just don't try and whack me on purpose.'

'Why would you think I'll do that?'

'Because you would,' Tayme replied weaving an emotional smile into his mind voice.

Trar flew low over the trees so that those walking below can see them coming and then flew ahead until she reached an opening in the trees big enough for her to land. She opened her tail feathers to help slow her speed and then banked and landed neatly in the middle of the path without hitting a single branch.

Tayme was impressed. Trar did not have much experience with landing in thick trees and she surprised him by handling them like an expert.

The tracker, Hanton, was the first out from the cover of the trees and he was not long after followed by Lieutenant Peana and the rest of the band.

"Did you sight anything Flyer?" The lieutenant asked the pair as Trar squatted to lower the distance between Tayme and the ground.

Tayme swung his leg over the saddle and slid down Trar's red, feathered shoulder to the road.

"Yes, sir. Trar thinks she's found a resting place of Adhamh further up the mountain."

"Any sign of humans?"

Tayme knew what the Lieutenant was asking but could not give him the information he needed.

"We did see evidence of human activity but it was made by a large group and the trail came from the direction of the Northern border."

The Lieutenant frowned.

"Arranians."

Tayme nodded. "That's what it looks like

Sir. And Trar saw some 'inconsistencies' in the clearing where Adhamh might have rested. Maybe he ran into that group and that's why he's gone."

"Or maybe, he and the Captain planned a rendezvous and that was their meeting point."

It was Tayme's turn to frown. Though his frown was more in disbelief at what he was hearing. Surely Peana could not have reached the rank of Lieutenant while being this stupid?

"And how would your Captain manage that?" Tayme asked. His voice was hard and sharp. "Adhamh cannot speak to him, and Captain Vosloo cannot hear him. A conversation between the Captain and Wing Commander Adhamh would be very one-sided."

"One-sided. Unless there was another Hatar pair that could act as an intermediary between them."

Tayme drew himself to his full height and Trar stood up on all fours and fluffed out her crimson feathers.

"Are you suggesting that Trar and I colluded somehow with your Captain?"

The Lieutenant stared hard at Tayme for a heartbeat more before turning his gaze away.

"No. No, I'm not." Dalon Peana ran a calloused hand through his hair. "I feel like we've been lead out under false pretensions and then left to our own devices. I don't like being used, and I don't like being left in the dark."

Tayme had to bite his lip. That was how every Kalar are treated all the time. At least the Kalarthri that were not Hatar Kalar could look forward to retirement and freedom after thirty years of Service. It would be nice to look forward to being pensioned off into a nice house and to be able to put your feet up whenever you want.

"Yes, Sir." Lieutenant Peana seemed like he was an okay kind of person in that he did not treat all Kalarthri like scum. But you can never be too careful. The face he is showing them now may be different to what he shows later. He may be one of those people who mould their values and words depending on what company they are in.

You get to experience all types of people when you are considered beneath anyone's notice. Tayme was still trying to make his mind up about which type of person Dalon Peana was.

"We had best go and have a look at this clearing then. But we will need to keep an eye out for any movement of Arranians. Whoever made the trail that the Hatar saw from the air is not worried about being seen or stopped in this area."

"So you think the Pydarki are colluding with the Arranians?"

"I don't know what to think. It's what the Captain was worried about before he disappeared. Either way, we need to check it out."

Tayme found himself waiting on the plateau with Trar as the scout group finally climbed their way into the clearing from the trees.

Tayme and Trar did spend their time productively as they waited for the rest of the company. They had found a lot of boot prints in the grass and dirt of the clearing. Near the tree line, they found the unmistakable impression marks of where a large Hatar had been lying sleeping. What was troubling about this was the number of booted footprints that surrounded it.

Once the tracker, Hanton, got here, he will need to take a good look and tell them what he thinks had happened.

There were a few long, black feathers littering the ground in this area which was all Tayme needed to tell him that they had found a resting place of Adhamh, confirmed by Trar when she snuffed at one of the long black feathers.

"Sorry we took so long," Hanton huffed as he stopped beside Tayme. "We have found plentiful signs of Arranian passage through the trees coming up to this clearing and going away again. They were leading something large when they were going away."

"Something large?"

'He's going to say something Hatar sized Kral.'

Tayme ignored Trar and stayed silent, waiting for the tracker to reply.

"I'll leave it for the Lieutenant to tell you. I'll take a look around here before the group starts to tramp out any evidence of what happened here."

Tayme nodded and Hanton went off to start his careful examination of the clearing.

'Do you think Adhamh went with the Arranians?'

'Not willingly he didn't. But what would make Adhamh go with them? Why didn't he fight to get away? How were they able to do it?'

'All very good questions which at the

moment we can't answer.'

As the tracker searched, the rest of his company came into the clearing and Lieutenant Peana made his way over to where Tayme and Trar stood by the edge of the plateau.

"What have you found?" he asked as he approached them.

"We think Adhamh retreated just under those trees, but it looks like something happened with a large group of men. We are waiting to see what your tracker can make of it. Trar scented a strange scent. They were not from the Empire."

"That makes sense. On our way up here, we found traces of a large group of men moving through the trees. Those tracks were left by an Arranian band."

The lieutenant glanced back towards the

trees where Hanton was hunched over.

"I am curious to see what he comes back with as well."

He turned back to look at Tayme.

"I think now would be a good time to break for lunch while we wait on Hanton."

"The best idea I've heard all morning," Tayme replied as Peana turned to shout orders to his men.

Once everyone was settled and eating, Hanton abruptly stood up near where the trees meet the cliff face and strode purposely towards them.

Trar was sprawled right on the edge of the cliff trying to warm herself in the noonday sun. Her raised head warned Tayme of the tracker's approach.

"Lieutenant," Tayme called as Peana had his

back to the trees.

Dalon Peana rose to his feet and turned to watch as Hanton walked to them with something clutched in his hand.

"What have you found?"

Hanton stopped and gave the lieutenant a brief salute before answering.

"A large company of Arranians were here and it looks like they ambushed a Hatar and secured him with ropes and chains." The tracker held out his hand which had a broken piece of rope with a metal hook attached and a broken piece of chain. "The creature put up a fight, but something stopped him cold. And he seems to have left with them."

"What would make a Hatar stop fighting and suddenly do what you want?" the Lieutenant asked, more to himself. But Tayme replied.

"They would stop fighting if the enemy held their rider."

"Are you suggesting that these are the people who might have taken your young Wing Commander?"

"It would be the only thing I can think of that would make Adhamh go anywhere with them without a fight."

Trar nodded her bright red head in agreement.

"Captain Vosloo was looking for her which might mean that he is not far behind. We need to follow them."

"I couldn't agree more," Tayme replied.

"I need you to get up into the air to see what direction they went, and then we will go hunting."

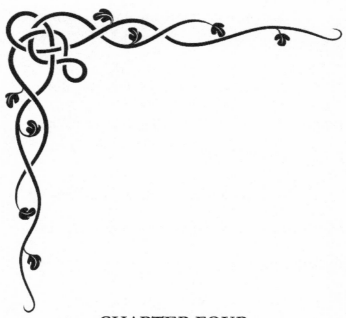

CHAPTER FOUR

THE DECISIONS

Foxtern was full of movement and
noise.

Wing Commander Harada stood just behind

Colonel Jan Oded as they watched a large company

of soldiers march out from the Muster Yards. There

had been a report of an Ice Tiger encampment half a

day's march North of Foxtern, and it had been decided to send a detachment of men to investigate.

And by investigate. Harada knew what was really meant was to exterminate.

Oded stood just under the overhang of his tent, Harada stood just within the entrance. He was with Oded this morning when the Colonel argued against this saying that more investigation was needed. Who could say that this was not a trap to get prisoners or to find out their strength in the area?

His concerns were brushed aside by the Justicar and his cronies. Captain Jerant sat and said nothing. He just had a stone cold look and expression on his face and his eyes did not leave those of Harada.

The last time they had met, it had not been

on good terms. In fact, he and Kalena were the reason Jerant was now at Fort Foxtern. And at the time Jerant made it clearly known that he did not like Kalarthri, especially the Hatar Kalar. Clearly, that dislike must have spread to the Justicars. It was their machinations that drew Jerant out an into the scheme of kidnapping a Pydarki.

Colonel Oded put forth his reasoning again for just sending flyers out to scout the camp and to see if any other Ice Tiger or Arranian activity could be detected.

Captain Jerant listened silently to Oded's argument and then listened to the Justicar's argument to send out a combined Justicar lead flyer/freeman force out to investigate.

But he did not go with either side.

He had already decided what they were to

do, and as the current ranking Commander at Fort Foxtern, as his own Commander had been called back to Hered, it was his decision to decide what to do. The forces assembled here were still waiting on final orders as to who exactly was in complete command of the Northern Army.

Harada was hoping it to be his brother, by rights it should have been Garrick, but for some reason, the Emperor has delayed issuing the writ conferring this as was traditional. But in the meantime, Captain Jerant was the ranking officer in command of the men permanently stationed at Fort Foxtern, and it was ultimately his decision on what should be done.

Jerant hated the flyers.

Jerant hated the Justicars.

And Jerant hated anyone who was allied

with Provost Marshall Brock.

Jerant was a person who was ruled by his emotions and currently that emotion was hate. Harada was curious as to what course of action the Captain would choose. Either choice would have him siding with someone he hates. His only problem will be weighing up who he has more.

Jerant sat straight in his chair, unmoving and emotionless. The lack of emotion worried Harada a little as it was so unlike the Captain. So when Jerant finally spoke he had everyone's attention.

"I do not think we have a need for flyers to go out. And I also see no need to have a Justicar to accompany the men. Fort Foxtern is going to send out an expeditionary company to the supposed Ice Tiger camp." Jerant turned his gaze to Oded and Harada. "We will see if what the Flyer saw is correct."

As people filed out from the meeting, Oded stayed behind. Jerant remained standing by his chair and Harada kept himself in the background, knowing his presence might antagonize Jerant.

"Captain Jerant. Are you sure it is wise to send those men out without aerial support? The flyers will be able to see the heat signs of those on the ground or hidden among the trees."

"Are you suggesting the men of Fort Foxtern can't do their duties without help?"

"No, but you should not refuse to use a tool that can be of use."

Jerant shook his head. "A tool needs to be reliable and trustworthy. The armies of the empire operated well enough for centuries without the Hatar Kalarthri. We do not need them now."

"You really hate them that much that you would risk your men?"

Jerant's face hardened and he starred long and hard at Oded.

"My men do not need the protection Kalarthri Flyers. As acting commander, I have made my decision. I do not need your liberal motives and agenda influencing my orders or the Freemen quartered here. Until the Emperor has made his decision as to who is in command, Provost Marshall Brock and any of his cronies have no power here." With that Jerant turned on his heel and strode from the room. He did not acknowledge Harada's presence. The Hatar Kalar was beneath his notice.

"You warned me what he would be like," Oded said without looking at the Hatar Kalar.

"You still had to go and experience it for yourself though," Harada replied as he stepped up next to Oded.

"That I did. And now I feel like I need a bath."

And now Oded and Harada watched as that force marched through the gates of Fort Foxtern and out into the wilds of the Bhaliger mountains.

"Jerant is a fool," Oded repeated for the umpteenth time.

Harada gave no reply. Oded was just giving voice to his frustration and he had been listening to him vent all morning.

"We could send out a flyer to keep an eye on

things," Harada eventually said.

"Jerant would know. He is watching us. Can't you see his underling a few tents down?"

Harada nodded. "I've seen him, though I thought he belonged to the Justicars."

"Doesn't matter who the man whispers to. He's reporting our actions to his master. Be that Jerant or Inman, the result will be the same."

"Felian will want to keep track of you especially and move against us to find out what we are doing."

"And as we are supporters of Garrick, we will be key people to discredit."

"You will be. I'm only a lowly Hatar Kalar. I am beneath notice," Harada replied with a laugh.

Oded turned to look at him.

"You may be a lowly Hatar Kalar Harada,

but your father still respects you."

Harada frowned.

"Seeing as how I haven't seen my father for over a year now, I can't see how that would worry anyone."

"You underestimate yourself and your importance Harada. You and your brother both do it. Garrick is heir to the throne and he needs to step up and take ownership of it."

"Why do you think he and Warrick have gone to Hered?" Harada replied a little stiffly. "They are the best placed to find out exactly what the lay of the land is there."

"Or get their heads removed from their stuck out necks," Oded muttered.

"All we can do is continue our search for Kalena." Harada moved forward to stand next to the Colonel in the doorway.

"We'd better. All Garrick's plans hinge on us finding that girl."

CHAPTER FIVE

NORTH

Dearen awoke in a cold sweat.

She sat up, letting the furs fall away from

her and the sudden touch of the cold morning air

made her shiver all the more.

A glance at the tent flap and the neatly

rolled blankets told Dearen that Hauga was already

up and was probably eating breakfast by the campfire.

But something was wrong. Something was very wrong.

The strange feeling she had before falling asleep the night before was now stronger and the urge to head North was pulling hard at her mind. Dearen had to consciously restrain the urge to move and to keep herself in her bedroll.

'Good morning Dearen. Nice to see you up.'

Dearen heard Hauga's mind voice. He must have felt some of her waking thoughts.

'Good morning Hauga. How is breakfast?'

'Excellent. Are you hungry?'

'Ravenous. Can you bring me something to eat?'

'You don't want to come out?'

'Not until I warm up a bit.'

'Okay. I'll be there with food shortly.'

'Just give me enough time to get dressed.'

'It's time like this that you wish you had fur like the rest of us don't you?'

'I just have to think about fleas and I'm thankful I don't.'

Dearen heard Hauga's chuckle and then there was silence.

Throwing off the furs, Dearen rolled off the bedroll and grabbed up her trousers and shirt. She was just pulling up her boots when Hauga appeared at the tent entrance, bringing with him the smell of beef stew.

Dearen's stomach rumbled in response.

Hauga ducked into the tent wearing a small

grin that showed his canines to good effect.

'At least your stomach is glad to see me.'

"My stomach is biased and only wants you for your stew."

Hauga shrugged his large shoulders.

'You have to take what you can get in this day and age.'

"I'll give you that. And I am glad that you are here. I need to talk to you about something."

Hauga's eye ridges shot up in surprise.

'Have I done something wrong?'

"No, no. Nothing like that. Here, sit with me on the bedroll and we'll eat as we talk."

Hauga nodded and handed Dearen the bowl as he lowered his large frame on the bedding next to Dearen. Both spent the next few moments eating in silence until Dearen rested her spoon in her bowl and turned to look up at Hauga.

"Something strange happened to me last night. Nothing bad mind you," Dearen added quickly as Hauga's feline features creased in concern.

"I had a strange feeling come over me. Or maybe it is more like a compulsion."

'What is it? What did you feel?'

"Something in my mind is telling me to head North. There is something North that I need to find, and that needs me to find it."

'Something wants you to find it?'

"That's the feeling it's giving me."

'Has this feeling told you what 'it' is?'

Dearen shook her head. "No, but whatever this is, it feels familiar to me. It feels 'right'. Something inside of me is responding and wanting to go."

Hauga's yellow eyes peeked at her from under their furry brows.

'So. You want to go North?'

Dearen took a moment to respond, to organize her thoughts and to 'get a read' on her internal gut feeling.

"Yes, I do. I think if I ignore it, it's just going to get stronger and stronger until I do what it wants."

Hauga looked back into his bowl as he twirled the stem of his spoon around between his clawed fingers.

'That's going to be a hard thing to do now that you are Cearc.'

"I know. With us confronting the Arranians and then maybe fending off those interlopers from the South, the Dymarki need their leader."

'Do you think this could be something that can help us keep our ancestral lands?'

Dearen shrugged. "I don't know Hauga. I don't know exactly what this is. I just know that it feels very familiar, like, a lost part of me that is trying to return home."

Dearen frowned and placed her bowl down on the floor.

"My gut feeling is that this could help me find out who I was before I woke up in that cave, and maybe tell me what had happened to me and why I have lost my memory."

'Or it could be something that takes you away from us Dearen.'

Dearen reached around as best she could and gave Hauga a hug. "I would never leave you

Hauga. You're my brother, and I would never leave my people, especially now that I am their leader. You took me in, no questions asked, looked after me and let me contribute to the clan as best I can. No one could ask for better than that."

'Thank you Dearen. But this might be something that you have no control over.'

"And the only way we'll know is if we go to find out."

'You've made up your mind to go then.'

"I suppose I have. And for all I know, this might be something that can help our people as well."

Hauga snorted.

'I don't have a good feeling about this Dearen. This is not a normal situation to be in. The Dymarki do not get strange feelings in their

heads to 'Go North'.'

"But I was not born a Dymarki Hauga. I am a Bareskin, a human, as you so elegantly pointed out to me this morning when I woke up.

'So you think this happens to Bareskins a lot then?'

Dearen shrugged. "I don't know. I can't remember my life before I woke up in your cave. All that I know this could be an everyday occurrence for Bareskins."

'Having weird feelings might explain why Bareskins are the way they are.'

Hauga tried to make his comment humorous but Dearen, for some unknown reason, felt a little offended. She tried not to let it show.

"Does that explain the way I am?" Dearen could not help but ask.

'I didn't mean you Dearen. You're one of us. You're my sister. You are Dymarki. You are The Cearc.'

"And as your Cearc. You must do as I command," Dearen shot back.

'The term is 'strongly suggest' but in essence. Yes. But you do not need to command me to help you. I am your brother, I would do nearly anything to help the family.'

"So you'll help me go north and find out what this 'feeling' wants me to find?"

Hauga nodded. *'Yes'*

"Excellent. Now we just have to work out how we are going to do this without leaving our people leaderless. Hopefully whatever this thing is that is calling me can be quickly found and we can get back home before anything can happen either with the Arranians or the Southerners or with Raga's clan. Otteran is a resourceful woman, I'm sure she can distract the people long enough to cover for us."

'I'll bring in Drusa to take temporary command of the Muster while we're away. He will be able to keep Raga and his people in line. If we are not gone for long, Drusa should be able to cover for us.'

"Don't worry Hauga. If we don't find what we are looking for within a week, then we will come back."

'The Council are not going to like you disappearing like this.'

"Raga and the others will have to learn to live with it. If I don't go than this feeling is going to keep growing in me until it drives me insane."

'When do you wish to leave?'

"As soon as possible. The quicker I find what this is, the quicker we can come back and defend our homeland."

Hauga stood up with his empty bowl and held his hand put to Dearen. She picked up her bowl from the floor and silently handed it to Hauga.

'I'll go and hand these in to get washed and then I'll get Drusa. He'll continue the training regime that you have planned. The rest of the clan will support him.'

"I'll begin packing as soon as we have informed Drusa what we are doing and what he and Otteren must do while we are away. Then we'll head north."

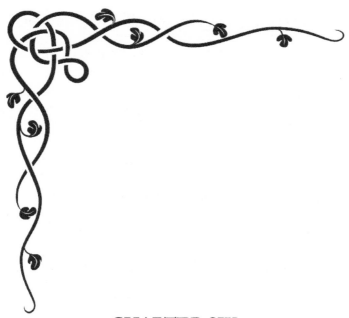

CHAPTER SIX

THE CLIFF

'They are loud.'

'Very. Can you smell anything?'

Dearen heard Hauga wuft a couple of deep

breaths.

'They don't smell like Arranians. But they

are Bareskins.'

Dearen felt a small twinge of relief that they were not Dymarki. Since they had left the camp that morning, she had been paranoid that once the Dymarki had discovered she had gone, that they would come after her. The fact that they have not means that Otteran and Drusa have been able to keep them secret.

'And they are heading in the same direction as we are?'

'Yes.'

Hauga and Dearen were on the edge of a small cliff that followed the bubbling stream they had run across. It was late afternoon and the two had decided to rest for a little while before pushing on to the north.

'They're obviously not Pydarki otherwise we wouldn't have heard them this far out.'

'No. The Pydarki are more surefooted than that.'

'That only leaves the Southerners then.' Dearen shifted her weight, they had been crouching in the brush ever since they had heard the first sound of movement and the long stay was making her muscles ache in protest. *'What has brought them this far into the Bhaligiers? Weren't they holed up in their place in the Southern pass?'*

Hauga shrugged. *'I have no idea. But whatever has brought them here cannot be good for us.'*

'I agree.'

A loud crunch echoed through the close-packed trees quickly followed by a soft curse. The group was close now. Dearen glanced up at Hauga.

'They sound like they are going to be

moving right beneath us if they keep to their current

path.'

Hauga gave a brief nod.

'Do we want to back away now or remain

hidden and wait for them to pass?'

'We wait for them to pass. That way we'll

get an idea of which way they are heading and then

make sure we don't follow them.'

'Good idea Hauga.'

Dearen and Hauga then hunkered down to

wait for these interlopers to pass by.

It was only a short wait before the first

Bareskin came into view along the edge of the

riverbank. He was quickly followed by several

more.

The first man was dressed in thick linens

and light leathers with a bow and quiver strapped to

his back. The others were dressed in thicker leather clothes and chainmail and were armed with swords and other blades. Clearly fighting men.

The last man out from the trees was dressed in finer attire and the hilt of his sword showed gilding but was utilitarian apart from that.

'An officer. Army men then.'

Dearen nodded. *'What are they doing this far north?'*

'Do you want to follow them?'

'No. We need to keep heading north ourselves. These men have posed no danger to us.'

'Yet!'

'Yet. If they had been Arranians then we would follow. But they are not and we need to keep focused on why we are out here and to get back home as soon as possible.'

'Yes, Cearc.'

'We'll wait, see where they go, and then continue on our journey.'

Hauga gave her a curt nod and turned his yellow eyes back to the men below them.

The group moved slowly (and noisily) along the creek bed and just as the group came to the widest point of the ground between the cliff face and the creek, the man at the back raised his hand and whistled.

All the heads before him turned back to look at him.

"It's getting late in the day. There is enough room for us all to camp comfortably here tonight. We'll stop, fill up our water canteens and set camp. I want us ready to be on our way again at first light."

The man then looked up at the open expanse of sky above them as if looking for something. Dearen glanced up as well but could see nothing. After a moment the man looked back to his motionless men.

"Well, get to it. And remember to leave room for Trar."

"Yes Lieutenant," they all called back before turning his words into action.

'Dearen. What now?'

'It looks like we'll either wait until nightfall to get away. Or if you think I'm good enough, we could try to make our way around them now.'

'I think it best we wait 'til nightfall. No offence, but you still need a lot of practice to be able to walk quietly in the woods.'

'No offence taken. I know my limitations

Hauga.'

Dearen looked down through the bushes to the men below. They had chosen the flat beach right below them and were busy setting a campfire and gathering water.

'We'll wait until they gather to eat their evening meal, then we'll move to get away from here.'

'Good idea. Bareskins are ruled by their stomachs, they will not be listening for your clumsiness.'

'Gee, thanks for the nice compliment Hauga.'

'What are brothers for?'

Dearen gave him a weak smile and then settled back to wait.

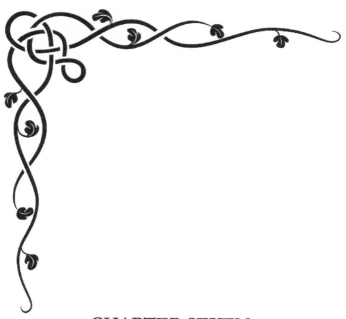

CHAPTER SEVEN

LOST FRIENDS

The sun was only a fingers width above the mountains to the west when the Bareskins below called out to the rest of the group that dinner was ready.

Dearen could smell the thick, meaty aroma coming from the contents of the pot from where they sat perched on the cliff top. It smelt like a thick, hearty stew and Dearen's mouth began to salivate. That pot smelt a lot better than the dry meat jerky that she and Hauga were looking forward to eating later that night.

'Let's make our move now while their attention is directed to filling their bellies.'

'We'll back away and then make our way north along the cliff.'

Dearen could see Hauga's slight nod of acknowledgement in the last light of the day.

The two backed away a good distance from the edge of the cliff making sure that they could not be seen by those below and started to make their way north, following the cliff and the river.

Keeping their attention focused on the Bareskin camp below them, they had barely gone beyond the cliff overhanging the camp, when Dearen heard a loud shout of alarm.

Both she and Hauga stopped instantly. The shout came from not that far ahead of them.

'Did you remember to count the people in camp?'

'No.'

'Neither did I.'

'We forgot to keep track of where all their sentries were set.'

'No use worrying about it now.'

Dearen still mentally kicked herself. It was such a trainee mistake.

'Let us just try to get away. The cry might not be about us.'

Dearen gave Hauga a sharp look which she knew Hauga's good low light vision could see.

'It might not be.'

'But most probably is,' Dearen mentally mumbled.

Noise from moving men coming from the camp was getting louder. Through the trees near the edge of the cliff, Dearen could now see the man who called the alarm. He was the first man they had sighted coming through the trees earlier that day and now he stood holding a loaded long hunting bow aimed in their direction.

'Do you see him?' Dearen asked.

'Yes I do,' Hauga responded.

'He can only hit one of us. Do you want to split apart? Or do you want to bull rush him?'

'Split. He'll see me as the bigger threat, the man will track me. It will give you the chance to jump him.'

'Agreed. We'll go on your mark Hauga.'

The whole conversation lasted less than a heartbeat and the two never took their eyes from the archer before them.

"Intruders on the cliff. Intruders! Come quickly," the man was now shouting. If they were going to do something, they had better do it before the men in that camp got up here to the cliff face.

'Go!'

Hauga's voice had barely finished in her head before she was off and running. She broke to her left and ran in a curve leading towards the archer. Just as Hauga predicted, the man's bow followed Hauga's large form through the trees to Dearen's right. His attention was away from her and she took advantage of it.

When Dearen judged herself close enough,

she jumped and landed hard on the man's back. She heard the whoosh as the breath was knocked from his lungs and Dearen's arm slammed down hard enough over his shoulder to snap the arrow that was drawn in the bow.

The now empty string on the bow shot forward and slapped the broken end of the arrow into his forearm.

Dearen locked her arms around his neck and her legs around his waist and used her weight to throw the lanky body of the man to the earth. She was ready for the ground so did not get her breath knocked from her. The man, on the other hand, began clawing at her arm across his windpipe. She was holding it tight enough to stop him yelling out but not tight enough to choke him.

Dearen responded by tightening the grip of

her legs around the man's waist, causing him to squeak in pain.

"Lay still and you won't get hurt. Do you understand?"

The man gave her a short nod and stopped his fighting, but kept his hands clutched to her arm, not ready to completely trust her word.

Hauga appeared out of the undergrowth and Dearen felt the man jolt with surprise. Dearen briefly tightened her arm as a warning not to move.

'You got him.'

'Obviously. Let's bind him and hide in the trees while his friends search the brush below us.'

'Gag him and hand him to me, I'll carry him up into the trees.'

"Don't move or make a sound," she said before moving her arm. Dearen pulled one of her scarves from around her neck and tied it around the

man's mouth as a gag. She then released the rest of

her grip and gave the man into Hauga's custody.

The Dymarki quickly picked him up, tucked him

over his shoulder and leapt up into the branches of

the tall trees around them.

Dearen scrambled up into the tree as the

sound of searching men came close to them as they

climbed up the cliff. She was not as nimble as

Hauga but was just as silent as she pulled herself up

to the branch beside him.

She plucked some leather cords from her

belt pouch and quickly bound the man's hands.

Dearen noted the man's wide, bulging eyes and the

flushed face covered with sweat staring back at her.

She watched as the eyes frowned and then focused

on the tattoo on her left cheek. Whatever he saw

calmed him down from his fright.

The noise of movement came from below and Hauga placed a warning hand on the man's shoulder. Dearen placed a finger to her lips to emphasize Hauga's warning.

She then peered down through the tree branches and saw flashes of men moving in and out of view, busy searching for their missing friend.

"Any sign of him?" Dearen heard someone call out.

"None," and "No," were the responses she heard given back. After a little more fevered activity the men moved away from their tree.

Dearen was about to let out a silent sigh of relief when a shout rang out from someone out of her field of vision.

"Lieutenant Peana. I've found something."

Dearen then caught sight of some men moving through the opening in the tree branches heading in the direction of the shout.

"A broken arrow. The fletching is Hanton's. No blood though."

A man came back into Dearen's view holding the end of a broken arrow in his hand.

"Everyone spread out and see if you can find any trace of what happened to him."

"Yes Sir," was echoed back to the man and the people mingling about him moved away heading out in all directions.

'What are we going to do Hauga? Those men are moving along our escape route.'

'We'll have to wait until they tire of searching.'

'What about our guest?'

'He seems pretty content at the moment. He seems completely fascinated by you. His eyes haven't moved off you since we've been up here.'

'Perhaps he hasn't seen a female in a while?'

'I can't say. But if he tries anything-'

'I know, you'll deal with him.'

Dearen kept her eyes focused on the man below her. This was the well-dressed man she saw earlier in the day. The leader of the group.

'The sky is beginning to darken. These Bareskins will stop their search soon and go back to camp.'

Dearen looked up through the sparse branches above them. They were very exposed to the sky here in the tree, and the soft blue of the daytime was slowly retreating, drawing the deep velvet dark of night across the sky.

'Once they go, we'll leave this man here and then go. They'll find him in the morning when they come to continue their search.'

Dearen turned her gaze to the man standing below quietly waiting, the broken arrow clutched tightly in his hand.

A loud high pitched screech pierced the air around them. The sound punched deep into Dearen's ears and she saw Hauga's mobile ears flatten hard against his head.

She looked up above and saw something big and silent pass over them, blocking the sky momentarily from her vision. Dearen's head whipped around as the loud crack of broken wood then cut through the woods and then heard something big moving in an area too constrained for it. Cries quickly came up from the men and the high pitched screech echoed up. This time it came from the direction of the trees and the shouting men.

'What was that?'

Hauga's ears were still flattened against his head and the fur all over his face and body was raised.

'That was something that we don't want to tangle with. That was a Hatar'le'margarten.'

'The thing that brought the rocks down on us in the mountain pass?'

'The same.'

'Whiskers! That's not good. Do you think it saw us?'

'There's a good chance it did. They have exceptional sight and smell.'

'Whiskers! And we are trapped up here in

this tree.'

Dearen looked at their prisoner who still did not look worried about his current predicament. In fact, he looked more happily excited than anything else.

The sounds of commotion below drew Dearen's attention back to the ground and she watched as the leader was quickly surrounded by his men and in the slowly darkening gloom a newcomer dressed in black appeared and headed directly to the trunk of the tree.

'Kalena, is that you?'

Dearen stilled in shock at the strange female voice that sounded in her head. For a moment she did not know what to do, but then her inner urge for action took over.

'Who is this?'

'It is you! Thank the One we found you

Kalena. This is Trar. Kral is coming to you now.'

'My name is Dearen, not Kalena. And if you

do not let me and my brother leave in peace, we will

harm the man we have with us.'

'Your brother? Is that Videan with you?'

'Videan? What? No!'

The conversation with Trar was confusing

and a headache was now starting at the back of her

head.

'What's wrong Dearen?'

Dearen held a hand up to Hauga for silence.

"You. Below. Let us leave in peace and we

will return you man unharmed."

The man in black suddenly looked up at her

excitedly before throwing a hand up to silence the

well-dressed leader.

"Kalena, is that you?"

Dearen closed her eyes and frowned. Not this again.

"My name is Dearen, not Kalena. What say you to my offer?"

The man seemed put out by her comment but quickly regained his composure.

"Of course you can come down. None here would harm you."

"What about my brother? What about him?"

"Your brother?"

"Hauga. My brother and my protector."

"Any friend of yours is welcome here Kalena."

'Dearen, no. You can't trust them,' Hauga said breaking Dearen's request for silence.

'There was that Kalena thing again. Maybe

we can use this to our advantage somehow.'

'I don't like it.'

'What else are we going to do?'

'I still don't like it.'

Dearen took the response as Hauga's concern and not a flat out no.

'At the first chance of escape, we'll take it.'

Hauga did not reply and his ears remained flattened against his head.

'Just remember, if they do try and double cross us, this power I have might come out and burn them all to a crisp.'

That comment brought an answering fang showing smirk on Hauga's face.

Dearen turned her attention back to the group now gathered around the trunk of the tree.

"Back away from the trunk and we'll come

down."

The men below slowly backed away from the tree trunk and Dearen gave Hauga a small nod before starting her descent from her tree branch. As she climbed down, she could hear the whispers of conversation flowing back and forth around her which felt familiar, like the feeling that brought them here. The voices were not like the Dymarki, so Dearen put up a stronger mental block to ignore them.

As soon as her feet hit the ground, her body tensed and she kept a wary eye on the men surrounding her. Especially the man in black who stood at the front of the men with the well-dressed leader.

A warning from Hauga and Dearen stepped forward as the body of their captive landed with a thud on the ground. Dearen kept her gaze focused on the man in black. He had a red mark spread across his face that caused a feeling of déjà vu in Dearen. She had the feeling that she had seen it before.

Dearen realized that Hauga had not yet come down.

"Get down here Hauga."

'Very well.'

She heard the creak of a branch and then felt Hauga's presence appear silently behind her. The men surrounding them quickly stepped back with cries and exclamations.

Dearen saw the leader turn to the man in black. "That is an Ice Tiger! Kral Tayme, what is going on here?"

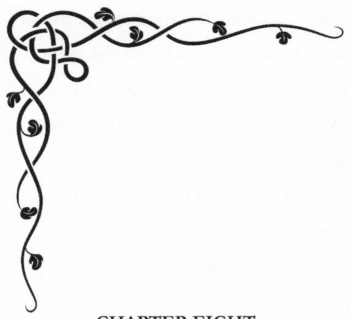

CHAPTER EIGHT

NOW FOUND

The man, Kral Tayme, held up a hand for silence, keeping his eyes focused on Dearen. "If you have patience, all things will be revealed Lieutenant Peana."

"So, what happens now?" Dearen asked the man called Kral Tayme.

"Kalena. It's me. Kral."

Dearen frowned. "I don't know you. And my name is Dearen."

Hauga moved forward and planted himself protectively next to Dearen. Gone was the fun-loving brother, now replaced with the serious bodyguard of the Cearc.

The soldiers around them immediately moved their hands to the hilts of their weapons.

"No. You are Kalena Tsarland. Wing Commander and paired with the Hatar'le'margarten Adhamhma'al'mearan. We have been out looking for you since you disappeared."

Dearen's frown deepened but said nothing in return. Asnar had mentioned nothing about this possibility.

The man took a step forward, encouraged by

Dearen's lack of response.

"Your best friend, Adhamh, has been taken by the Arranians. We are tracking them north and hope to catch up to them soon. It will be a nice surprise for Adhamh to see you with us when we rescue him."

Dearen and Hauga glanced at each other at the mention of Adhamh moving north.

'Maybe that is why you are being drawn to the north?' Hauga said.

'Maybe. It depends on when he was taken.' Dearen turned back to Tayme.

"When was this Adhamh taken by the Arranians?"

"A day or so ago."

'It matches up then. Maybe it is this Adhamh calling for you,' Hauga said.

'But why doesn't he just speak to me like you do?'

'Just like sound, our mind voices cannot be heard over long distances Dearen.'

'Yeah, I know. But I thought Hatar'le'margarten were these 'all powerful' mind mages'.'

'They might not be as powerful as they once were Dearen.'

'That is true. They might not be,' she agreed. *'But, if they are going in the same direction as us, maybe we can travel with them a little.'*

'Dearen, they will not travel freely with me. Look at them. They are itching to run their blades through me.'

'But they have given their word that they wouldn't.'

'Would you trust the word of strangers after what we have witnessed of Bareskins so far?'

'But these are southern Bareskins. Not Arranians. We'll take a chance. What other choice do we have?'

'None. But remember that this chance you are taking involves me keeping my life.'

Dearen gave Hauga a nod. Their conversation had lasted no more than the blink of an eye and the man, Kral Tayme, was waiting for her reply.

"I have your word, and the word of everyone here that Hauga will not be harmed?"

"He will not be harmed-" The officer, Peana, cut off Tayme's reply by grabbing him roughly on the shoulder and spinning him around. After a hurried but heated conversation, the officer reluctantly nodded his agreement. Tayme turned back to Dearen.

"He will not be harmed as long as he shows no aggression towards us."

"Hauga will only attack if you threaten him or me." Dearen looked at Hauga who gave her a brief nod. "Very well. We will surrender to you and entrust our lives into your care."

Dearen drew her sword and handed it hilt first to Tayme.

"Don't be silly Kalena. You can keep your weapons. Your friend on the other hand…"

Dearen looked at Hauga quizzically. "As you can see, he does not carry any hand weapons."

Tayme gave Hauga a quick look up and down before letting his gaze linger on the Dymarki's big hands tipped with razor-sharp claws.

The sharp fangs did not help Hauga's case either.

"He does have his natural weapons and those he will very definitely not be giving up."

"So I see," Tayme replied. "Very well. Agreement accepted." Tayme spat on the palm of his hand and then held it out towards Dearen.

Dearen looked at the hand and then up at Hauga.

'What am I supposed to do with that?'

The Dymarki shrugged.

'I don't know. Maybe he wants you to spit on it as well.'

Dearen was drawing her breath to do just as Hauga said when the man must have realized her confusion.

"Here, you need to shake my hand to make the deal binding."

Dearen felt a stir of revulsion in the pit of her stomach, but she swallowed it down before spitting into the palm of her right hand and clasping it firmly to Tayme's.

"Deal is made."

"Excellent. Now we can release Hanton from those bindings and get back to camp so we can all eat what is now probably burnt in those camp pots."

CHAPTER NINE

FOOD AND SLEEP

Dearen spent the night curled up next to

Hauga. The comfort of his warm fur allowed her to

go over the events of the day in her mind. They

were surrounded by these unknown Bareskins and

at the far end of the riverbank slept the red

Hatar'le'margarten that had flown over them

earlier.

Kral Tayme was the name of the man in black and he was the rider of the red Hatar who she learned was called Trar. He had spent a large portion of the evening talking to her about this Kalena person. Hauga sat quietly next to her, keeping an eye on all the men about them. The men about them returned the favor.

Lieutenant Peana, who was in charge of the men sat across from them listening and adding his own comments when needed. Apart from that, he did not say much else.

A lot of what Tayme spoke of just washed over her. And it was not his words that made Dearen begin to think that Tayme, maybe, was speaking the truth. Hauga noted that Tayme carried the same mark on his face that she did. It was then that she really looked at him and saw the black leaping ram tattoo on his face.

When she asked about it, Tayme said that it was the mark of a Flyer and that she was one too and that her Hatar partner had disappeared while looking for her.

Dearen did not know what to think of this information. Except that the mention of Adhamh's name struck an answering chord with the feeling in her head.

That tattoo on Tayme's face did more to convince her of Tayme's tale than anything that he actually came out of his mouth.

She was relieved when eventually Tayme and Dalon Peana had taken their leave of her to go to sleep. At the far end of the camp, she could see the cold glint from the red Hatar's eyes as she surveyed the camp.

They had no chance to leave the camp without the Hatar giving the alarm if they so decided. Dearen and Hauga found a space just outside of the ring of firelight and laid out their bedrolls.

Hauga and Dearen then fell into a restless sleep. Well, Dearen did at least. She knew that Hauga would most probably stay awake not really trusting the strange bareskins around them.

But during the night, Dearen decided what they would do. This Bareskin group's goals coincided with her own. So she and Hauga will travel with them until they can get cleanly away from them. Or if they find this Hatar 'Adhamh,' she can find out if this feeling in her head actually was connected to him.

She awoke to Hauga's hand on her shoulder.

'Did I fall asleep?' Dearen asked as she yawned.

'Yes, you've had more sleep than I've had. And knowing your belly, it will be growling for something to eat shortly.'

As if on cue, Dearen's stomach began to rumble. She gave the Dymarki a weak smile.

'We'd better go and eat. Try not to insult the Bareskins about their food, if we have to travel with them I want it to be congenial.'

Hauga wrinkled his nose. *'It's going to be tough, their food smells simply horrendous. But I'll hide my revulsion to it for you Cearc.'*

'That's all a leader can ask Hauga,' Dearen said with a smile. Her brother always knew exactly what to say to make her feel better.

116

After a short breakfast, the group left the riverbank camp and continued heading north.

Dearen and Hauga walked in the middle of the group, and Tayme and the Hatar Trar left them to scout out the way ahead from the air while the man, Hanton, was sent to scout out the trail ahead. But during the morning, Dearen would hear Trar's voice asking her if she was okay and if she really could not remember anything about Adhamh at all.

The fact that she could not remember any of them at all seemed to bother the Hatar. Dearen shrugged that away. Her thoughts as they walked were more focused on what would happen to her, and the Dymarki, if what Tayme told her was true and that she was this Kalena Tsarland.

As far as she was concerned, nothing would change. She is the Cearc, the leader of the

Dymarki, that is who she is now, at this point in time. Whatever she was before cannot change that.

'You never know Dearen. This might help a peace treaty between the Southern Bareskins and the Dymarki.'

'It might. But that does not help us with the Arranians.'

'No, but it might stop the Southern Bareskins from attacking our rear while we are dealing with the Arranians.'

'True. Or they may sign a treaty with us and betray us anyway.'

'Dearen!'

'Hauga. Not all people are like the Dymarki. That much I do remember. Most are good but some are bad. Very bad'

Hauga gave her a small shrug. *'This lot*

seem okay though. Maybe we might have a chance

at getting our homeland back. We can't pass up a

chance of that happening without a fight.'

Dearen gave him no reply and focused her attention on the hike north. The further they moved, the stronger the feeling in her head grew. Now instead of being a feeling, it was more of a living presence. Dearen had the sense that it was trying to communicate with her, but something was blocking it. The scar tissue behind her ear had gradually started to itch as if there was something there trying to grab her attention. She rubbed it with her fingers, but the sensation persisted.

'What will you do if you are this Kalena?' Hauga suddenly asked.

Dearen turned and gave him a hard stare while she rubbed hard at her scar. If she did not know any better, she would think the Dymarki was scared.

'No matter what they say Hauga, or who I turn out to be. At the moment I am Dearen, Cearc of the Dymarki, and I am your sister. That will not change unless you or the Dymarki disown me.'

'And that will not happen Dearen. We swore an oath that binds us until death, no matter who you are or what you do, that will never change.'

'Thanks, Hauga.'

'If what they say is true, that means that this Adhamh they are looking for is a Hatar'le'margarten. Imagine, the Cearc riding a Hatar'le'margarten. That would be enough to put the Fear of Flattu into anyone who opposed us.'

Dearen tried to stop the snigger that the

comment brought to her lips but ended up sounding like a pig snorting. That then made her and Hauga burst out laughing which startled the already uneasy men around them. She did not care. The laugh made her feel good and helped to dispel the confused feelings that were pushing to be heard in her mind.

It was not long after that Trar and Tayme appeared in the sky flying back towards them, and for once the Hatar was not trying to talk to her.

As soon as Dalon Peana was made aware, he stopped the group to wait. Trar turned on a wingtip and landed on the path ahead in an open area that could accommodate her size. Tayme did not dismount, and as soon as Peana and the rest of the group were within earshot he called out. "There is a camp off to the north from here that has been attacked."

Hauga looked at Dearen with a startled look and then pushed forward with a snarl, causing the men around him to go for the hilts of their swords. Dearen followed him and placed a hand on his arm to calm him.

'They can't understand you. Let me talk,' she told him. She then turned to Tayme.

"That is a Dymarki camp. We had friends there. Do you know if they are okay?"

Tayme looked to the Lieutenant, who nodded his permission to talk.

"Trar did see some Ice Tiger bodies but we could not see who did the attack or where they had gone from there."

"We've got to go Dearen. If there are survivors we need to help them.'

"Yes we do," she replied quietly. Louder to the group she said. "Hauga and I are heading to the camp. You can choose to follow us or not, but it is probably a good bet that this was done by the Arranians. And if you are looking for a group, this could be them."

"You both need to stay here with us," the lieutenant cut in.

Dearen looked the man square in the face. "We are going and we will travel quicker by ourselves than with you. If you want us then follow because the only way to stop us going is to kill us."

"Kalena. Don't," Tayme called down. "I'll fly with them and Trar can keep an eye on them. We'll assess the area before you arrive. If there are survivors it would be better for an Ice Tiger be the first to enter the camp rather than one of our own

123

men."

Dalon Peana thought on Tayme's words a moment. "Very true." He turned and looked around at his men as if gauging their mood before turning back to Tayme. "You fly with these two and we'll follow."

"Yes, Sir."

As soon as Hauga and Dearen heard the assent they took off running into the trees. Behind them, they heard the rustle of feathers and the sound of wings sweeping through the air as the Hatar leapt up into the sky.

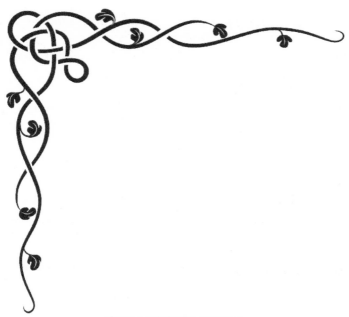

CHAPTER TEN

THE CAMP

Hauga in his concern began to outdistance
Dearen, forgetting that she was still only human.
She called out to him and he slowed a little to help
her move.

'Hauga, is this the camp I think it is?'

'Yes. This is the camp where you woke up

after the Pydarki gave you into our care. This is where we first met.'

'Then that means…'

'Then that means that the people there are our Clans people, our family.'

Dearen said no more, wanting to use all her concentration in moving her body forward as quickly as possible. Who could have done such a thing? It has to be the Arranians. They came and killed the old Cearc and a good number of the Clans people, and now they are going to systematically clear out all of the camps, even though this is not in Arranian held territory.

Dearen ran but in her heart, she was dreading what she may – will – find there. These are friends. The first friends she could remember. They are her family.

She signaled to Hauga to not wait for her and with not much more urging, Hauga took off, disappearing into the trees and undergrowth. Dearen continued on as fast as she was able. Her heart thudded quickly against her ribs and each intake of breath felt like a searing pain in her lungs as her stressed and exerted body cried out for more oxygen.

A snarl reverberated from the trees ahead of her. Hauga must have arrived at the campsite. Dearen pushed herself harder to join him. She began to recognize some of the landscape about her and as she broke through the final ring of trees, Dearen stopped dead in her tracks.

The cave mouth beckoned to her from the far end of the encampment, an old fire pit stood cold in the center. Everywhere else was covered in bodies.

There were no fires lit and everywhere was cold and silent and the food was left untouched in cook pots and platters. No one was moving and Dearen could hear – nothing. Nothing except Hauga's rumbling.

A few of the Dymarki was sitting upright against the stone entrance to the cave. The rest lay on the ground, slain either where they sat or stood.

The Dymarki were the only dead. Whoever did this must have descended upon them so quickly that the camp had no chance to react, or came in such numbers that they were able to carry off their dead when they left.

Hauga moved from body to body checking for any sign of life, his growling growing louder and louder with each friend he saw.

Tayme came in from the other side. Trar must have landed in the open area near the river. The sight of the Southerner knocked Dearen out of the shock she was experiencing from all this death. She quickly moved forward and began to check the dead that Hauga had not seen yet. Each face was known to her and Dearen felt her anger rising higher at each new lifeless face that stared sightlessly back at her.

'This is unforgivable,' she said to Hauga.

'This needs to be paid back in blood. They had been caught by surprise, given no chance at defense. They were slaughtered.'

'It must have been the Arranians. This is my fault. They did it straight after I sent them our challenge. This is my fault.'

'No. How were you to know that they would

react like this? Instead of meeting us in open

combat, they want to attack us like bandits.'

    'I should have known this would happen

after what they did at Councilmeet.'

    'Dearen-'

    'They are the ones who started this, but we

are going to be the ones who finish this.'

    "Kalena."

The voice tore Dearen's attention away from

Hauga and her eyes focused on Tayme who now

stood in front of her.

    "Kalena."

Dearen's eyes narrowed at the name as she

rose from the final body. "My name is not Kalena.

It is Dearen."

    Tayme held his hands up in an effort to

deflate the situation. "I'm sorry. Dearen. I wanted

to see if you were okay."

"Me? I am fine, but The Lord of Winds help whoever did this when I find them."

Hauga now stood next to her and gave a growl of agreement. Tayme took an involuntary step backwards at the sound.

'They are all dead, though whoever did this may have taken captives.'

"The Arranians have never taken captives before, what makes you think they have now?"

'There are two missing who should be here. Unless they are lying further afield, then they have been taken.'

"We need to get them back."

"What is going on?" Tayme asked.

Dearen turned her attention back to him. She had momentarily forgotten that he cannot hear their talk even though he could hear Trar's mind talk.

"Hauga had just told me that there are two missing from the camp. That they may have been taken by whoever attacked here."

Tayme glanced up at Hauga's stony face and then back at Dearen. "You're thinking of going after them aren't you?"

"There is no 'think' about it. We are. Why?"

Tayme gave a small smile. "It's just something that you would do. You're always helped friends in trouble."

"Did you see any sign of their passage from where you entered?"

Tayme shook his head. "Trar did not see anything but she can't see through the thick trees.

Not even the heat signatures can be seen through the thick canopy here."

'I'll go and scout around the camp outskirts to see if I can find out which direction they have gone.'

"Yes, go before the wind covers the tracks."

Hauga gave her a small sniff and moved off into the surrounding trees. In the far, far distance came the faint sound of the rest of their group coming through the trees. Dearen did not plan on waiting for them once Hauga had finished his track.

'Dearen, someone is coming in from the North. They are not Dymarki.'

"Hauga says that there is someone coming," Dearen told Tayme and drew her sword as she turned to the North. She heard the sound of metal as Tayme did the same.

A few moments passed and then Dearen heard Hauga's voice again.

'Ah, it is that tracker we captured. Hanton. He is excited about something. I'll follow him in.'

Dearen released the breath she had been holding and sheathed her sword.

"It's Hanton."

Tayme slid his sword back in its scabbard and took a few steps forward. "He was scouting ahead of our group. He must have found something to make him come back to find us."

A few heartbeats later, the tracker entered the clearing and suddenly stopped at the sight of the carnage.

"What happened?" he asked wheezing.

Tayme followed his gaze around the camp. "We were just trying to work that out ourselves.

The camp was like this when we got here."

Hanton nodded and then stood a few moments trying to catch his breath enough to talk. "Where is Lieutenant Peana?"

Tayme jerked his head to the block of trees behind him. "He and the rest of his men are still coming. Why?"

The tracker looked at Tayme a moment and then stared at Dearen. After a brief moment of indecision, he blurted out. "I have found an Arranian camp to the north of us."

"That must be the same group that did this!"

"AND they have a black Hatar with them held captive."

"You've found Adhamh?" Tayme stepped forward, not able to tame his excitement. "How far away?"

"They are not far, maybe just under an hour's walk north," Hanton panted as he pointed out the direction.

"What are their numbers?" Dearen asked quickly, worried that Hanton may quickly clam up and wait for the lieutenant.

"The Arranians number about fifteen to twenty men as far as I could tell. They have the Hatar chained and roped at the northern end of their camp. At least three of the men there are high ranking, and one wore the robes of a Spellcrafter."

'Spellcrafters!' Hauga's voice boomed in surprise and maybe a little fear.

"They have Spellcrafters with them?" Tayme could not keep the disbelief from his voice.

"It looks like it," Hanton replied a little defensively.

"That might explain why there was not much of a fight when they captured Adhamh."

"We are going to have to think of a way to neutralize the Spellcrafter if they have one," Dearen said.

'Kill them. You can't trust them alive.'

"Maybe Hauga, but we will have to think of a way to take them out first before the rest of the group can react."

'The only way to plan that is to go to their camp, study them, see if there are Spellcrafters and then act.'

"I agree." Dearen quickly took a breath to address Tayme and Hanton. "Hauga and I have decided to head to the Arranian camp and we are going with or without you. Though we would prefer you with us to help us out with numbers.

Hanton, did the group look like it was going to stay put for a while?"

"Yes. They had tents up and the Hatar was pretty well chained up. They are not going to be moving in a hurry. It looks like they have made a semi-permanent camp. Maybe that's why this one was attacked. It was too close to theirs."

"Doesn't matter why they did it. It just matters that we make them pay for all these deaths."

Hauga came out from the trees and stood like a giant sentinel stone. Waiting.

"We are going. Tayme, you and Trar can follow us, but you may want to stay out of sight of the Arranian camp. If they can take one Hatar, they might be able to take another. Hanton, stay here and wait for the others. Tell them what we are doing and if your Lieutenant decides to follow, try and find us at the southern end of the Arranian camp."

The tracker gave a weak nod before gulping loudly.

"Trar and I will follow and we'll watch out for the Spellcrafter. If we can take them out, then Trar can handle the rest."

"Right. Our plans are made. Let's set about making them happen."

To Be Continued in

Part 7

The Whisperer

Get The Way to Freedom: The Complete Season
One (Books 1-5)
This collection contains the complete first season of
the epic fantasy saga, The Way to Freedom - all
FIVE debut season episodes. Save 40% versus
buying the individual episodes!

**Thank you so much for reading and I hope to see
you again.**

Thank you for reading my book. If you enjoyed it,
won't you please take a moment to leave me a
review?

THE KALARTHRI

The Way to Freedom, Book One

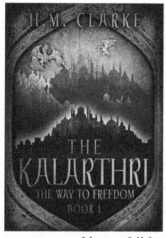

"This Hatar Kalar has more natural Talent than any Second Born found in the Empire."

Every ten years the Imperium Provosts travel the provinces of the Great Suene Empire and take every second born child as the property of the Emperor. His Due for their continued protection.

Kalena, taken from her family and friends finds herself alone and scared in the imperial Stronghold of Darkon. And when she cries out to the darkness for help, Kalena is shocked when it answers her back.

If you found out that you were different from everyone else, what would you do?

HOWLING VENGEANCE
John McCall Mysteries, Book One

John McCall just wanted to get a surprise for his men. Instead he got a disemboweled body.

A man is arrested for the murder but McCall is sure that they have the wrong person.

And when McCall starts digging around for the truth, he unearths a whole lot more than he bargained for.

Howling Vengeance. A supernatural mystery in the Old West.

Available now at your favorite Online Bookseller

THE ENCLAVE

The Verge, Book One

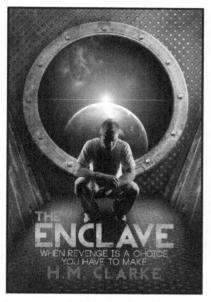

Katherine Kirk lived only for vengeance.

Vengeance against the man who destroyed her home, her family and her life.

Sent on a babysitting mission to Junter 3, RAN officer Katherine Kirk, finds herself quickly embroiled in the politics between the New Holland Government and the Val Myran refugees claiming asylum.

After an Alliance attack Kirk and her team hunt the enemy down and discover that they have finally found the lair of the man they have been searching for…

And the captive who has been waiting patiently for rescue.

"What would you do to the man who destroyed every important person in your life?"

Winter's Magic

Book One of The Order

Kaitlyn Winter is biting at the bit to become an active agent for the Restricted Practitioners Unit. And on her first day in the job she is thrown into a virtual s**t storm (to put it nicely).

First, she gets targeted for Assassination by The Sharda's top assassin

Second, her Werewolf best friend decides that her being 'Straight' means she can't protect herself and places her in protective custody

Third, the love of her life still won't notice her existence and the Tempus Mage who's set to keep an eye on her is infuriatingly attractive….

You can find out more information and sign up for Hayley's monthly newsletter on her website http://www.hmclarkeauthor.com/

ABOUT THE AUTHOR

In a former life, H M Clarke has been a Console Operator, an ICT Project Manager, Public Servant, Paper Shuffler and an Accountant (the last being the most exciting.)

She attended Flinders University in Adelaide, South Australia, where she studied for a Bachelor of Science (Chem), and also picked up a Diploma in Project Management while working for the South Australian Department of Justice.

In her spare time, she likes to lay on the couch and watch TV, garden, draw, read, and tell ALL her family what wonderful human beings they are.

She keeps threatening to go out and get a real job (Cheesecake Test Taster sounds good) and intends to retire somewhere warm and dry – like the middle of the Simpson Desert. For the time being however, she lives in Ohio and dreams about being warm…

You can find out more information and sign up for Hayley's monthly newsletter on her website –
http://hmclarkeauthor.com
http://eepurl.com/SPy61

Or catch her on Twitter - **@hmclarkeauthor**

Made in the USA
Las Vegas, NV
28 February 2021

18792099R00090